Duck, Duck, Porcupine!

Salina Yoon

BLOOMSBURY

NEW YORK LONDON OXFORD NEW DELHI SYDNEY

For Lily and Tansy, with love!

First published in the United States of America in May 2016
by Bloomsbury Children's Books
Paperback edition published in September 2017
www.bloomsbury.com

Bloomsbury is a registered trademark of Bloomsbury Publishing Plc

For information about permission to reproduce selections from this book, write to
Permissions, Bloomsbury Children's Books, 1385 Broadway, New York, New York 10018
Bloomsbury books may be purchased for business or promotional use. For information on bulk
purchases please contact Macmillan Corporate and Premium Sales Department at
specialmarkets@macmillan.com

The Library of Congress has cataloged the hardcover edition as follows:
Names: Yoon, Salina, author.
Title: Duck, Duck, Porcupine! / Salina Yoon
Description: New York: Bloomsbury Children's Books, 2016.
Summary: Big Duck likes to boss around her younger brother, Little Duck, and she fancies herself the leader
of their trio when joined by their gentle friend Porcupine. Little Duck does not speak yet, but through his
expressions and his actions, he shows that he has a better grasp on any situation than his older sister.
Identifiers: LCCN 2015022813
ISBN 978-1-61963-723-8 (hardcover) • ISBN 978-1-61963-812-9 (e-book) • ISBN 978-1-61963-869-3 (e-PDF)
Subjects: | CYAC: Ducks—Fiction. | Brothers and sisters—Fiction. | Porcupines—Fiction. | BISAC: JUVENILE FICTION/
Animals/Ducks, Geese, etc. | JUVENILE FICTION/Social Issues/Friendship. | JUVENILE FICTION/Family/Siblings.
Classification: LCC PZ7.Y817 Du 2016 | DDC [E]—dc23
LC record available at http://lccn.loc.gov/2015022813

ISBN 978-1-61963-724-5 (paperback)

Art created digitally using Adobe Photoshop
Typeset in Cronos Pro
Book design by Salina Yoon and Colleen Andrews
Printed in China by Leo Paper Products, Heshan, Guangdong
5 7 9 10 8 6 4

Three Short Stories

One
A Perfect Day for a Picnic

Two
I Think I Forgot Something!

Three
The Campout

One

A Perfect Day
for a Picnic

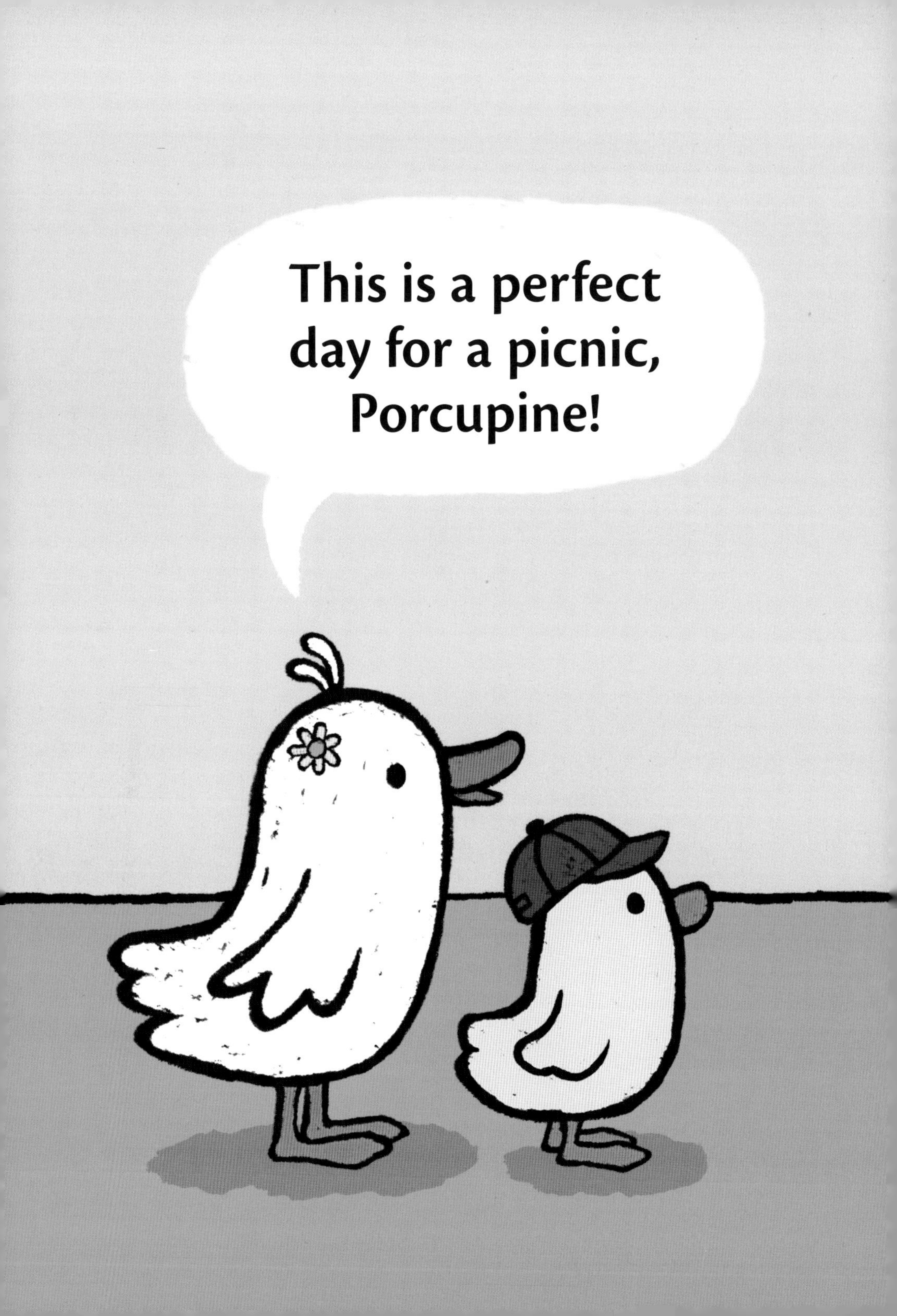
This is a perfect day for a picnic, Porcupine!

Yes it is, Big Duck!

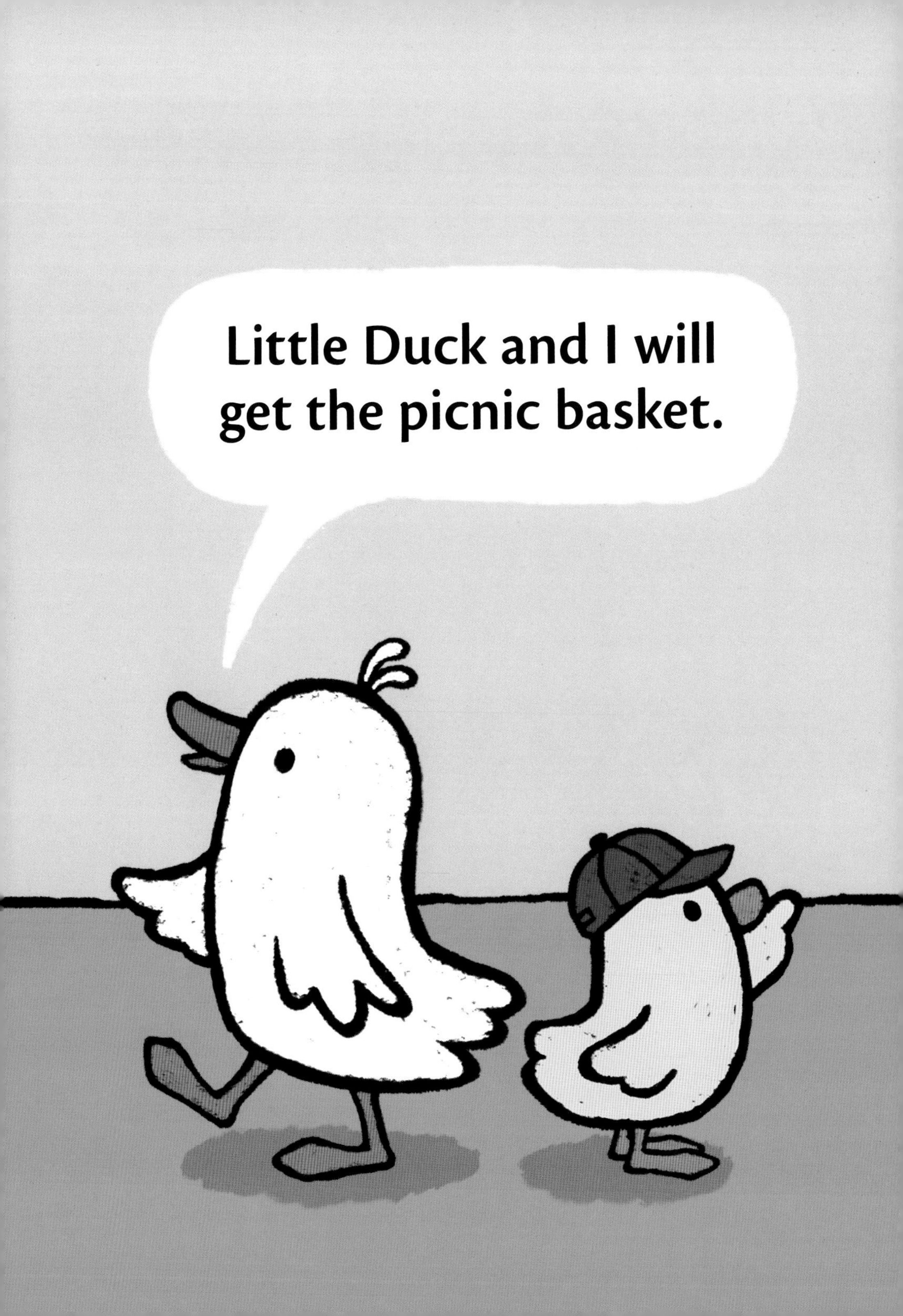
Little Duck and I will get the picnic basket.

I will get the
picnic blanket.

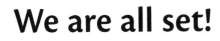

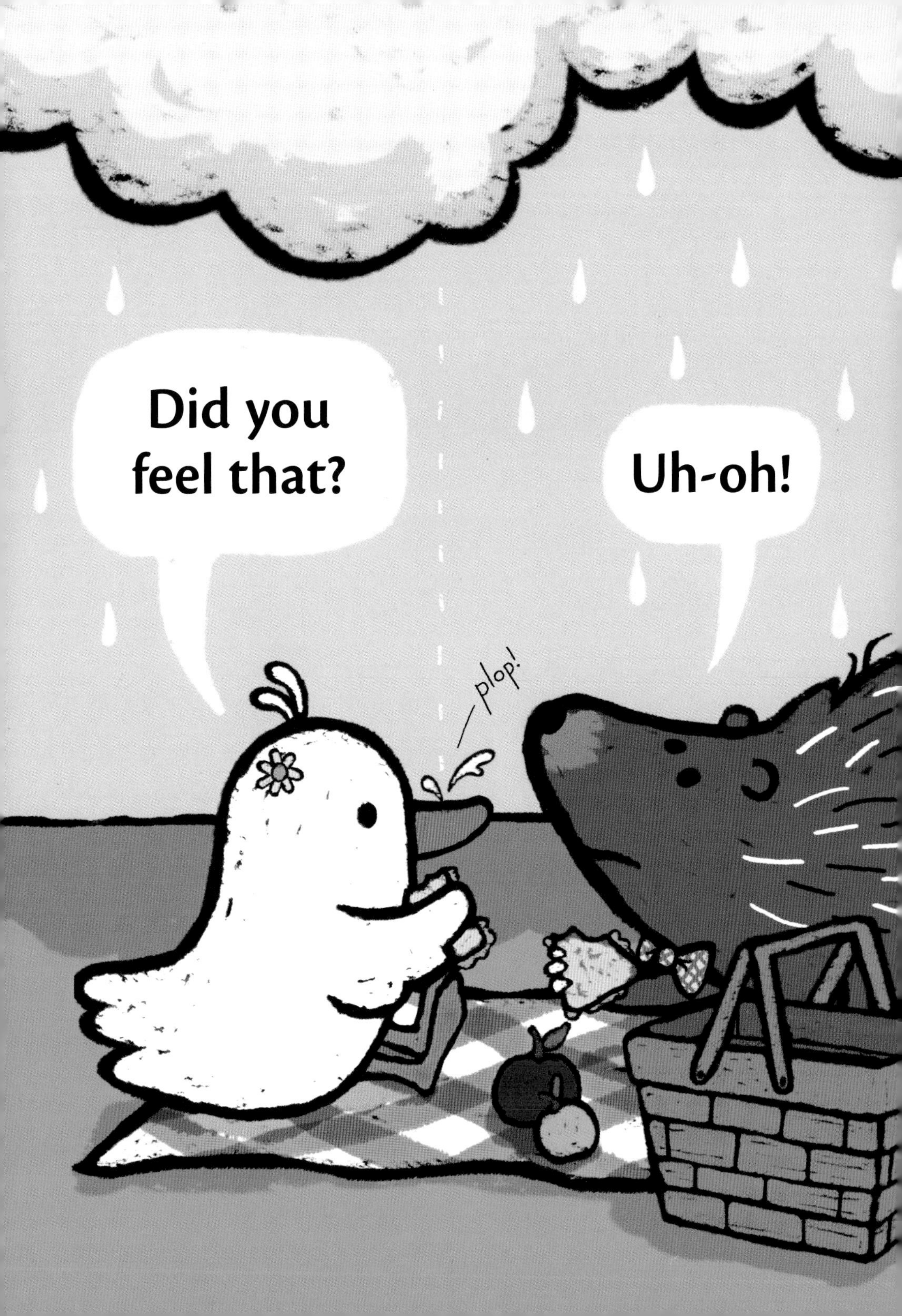
Did you feel that?
Uh-oh!
plop!

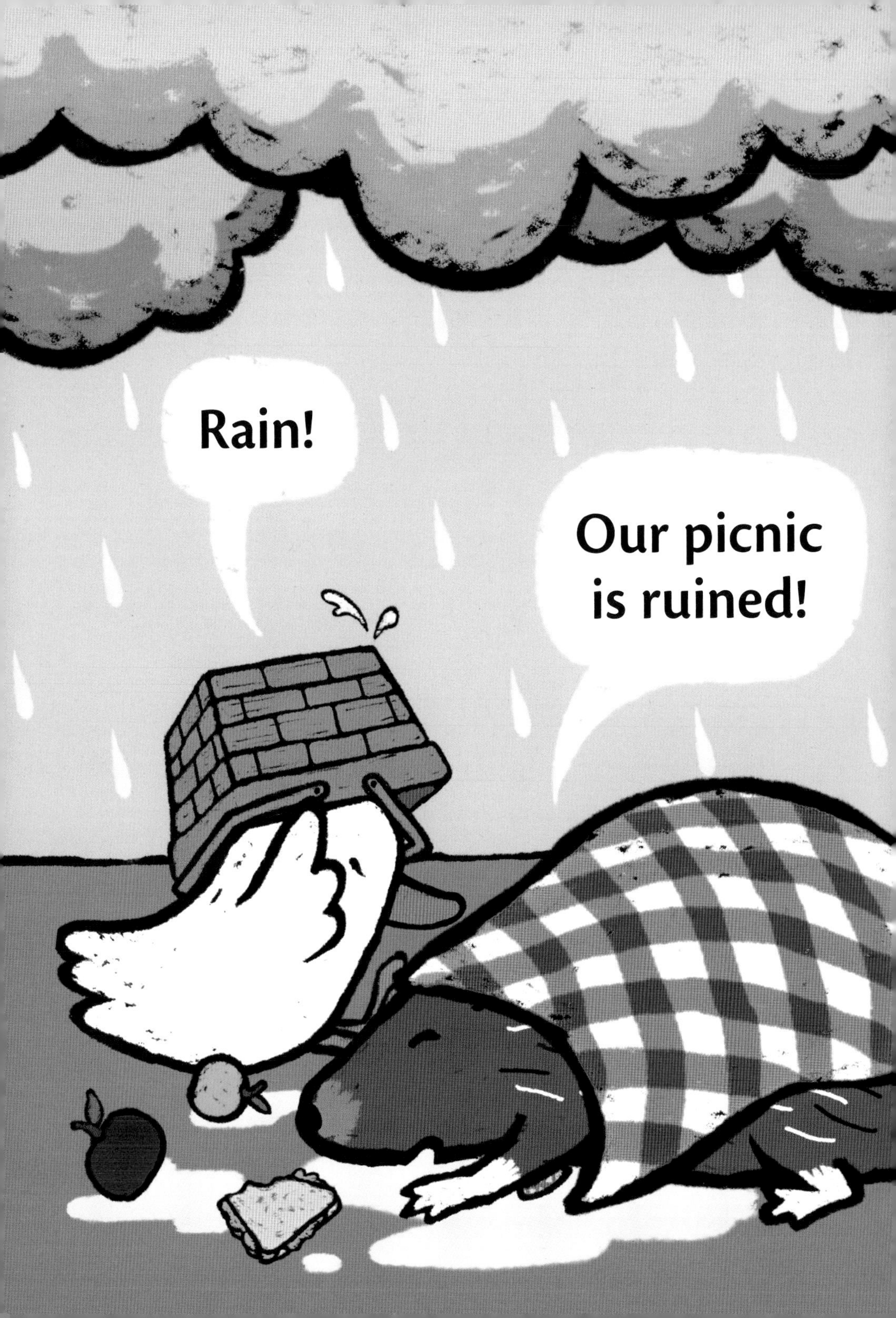
Rain!
Our picnic is ruined!

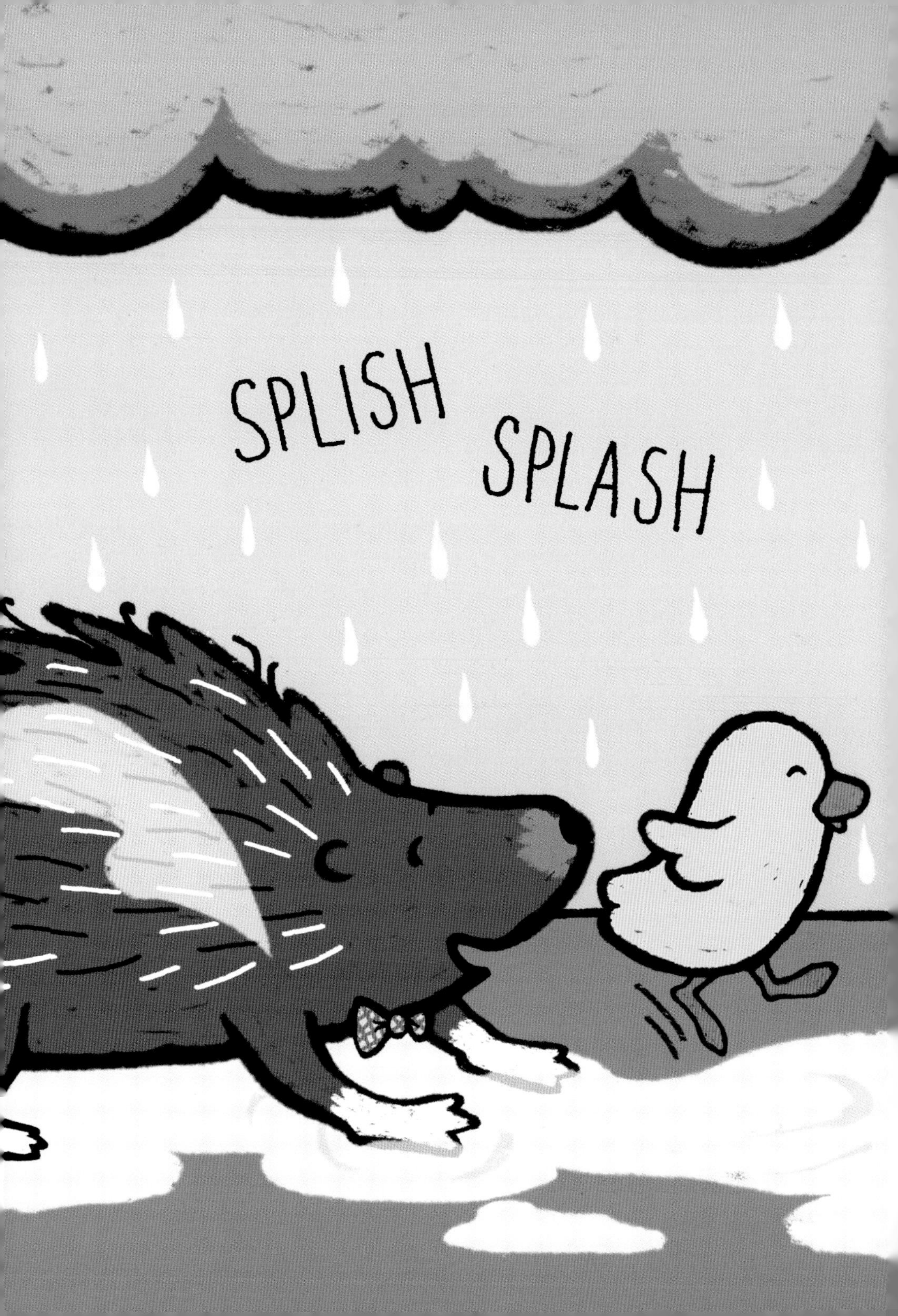
SPLISH
SPLASH

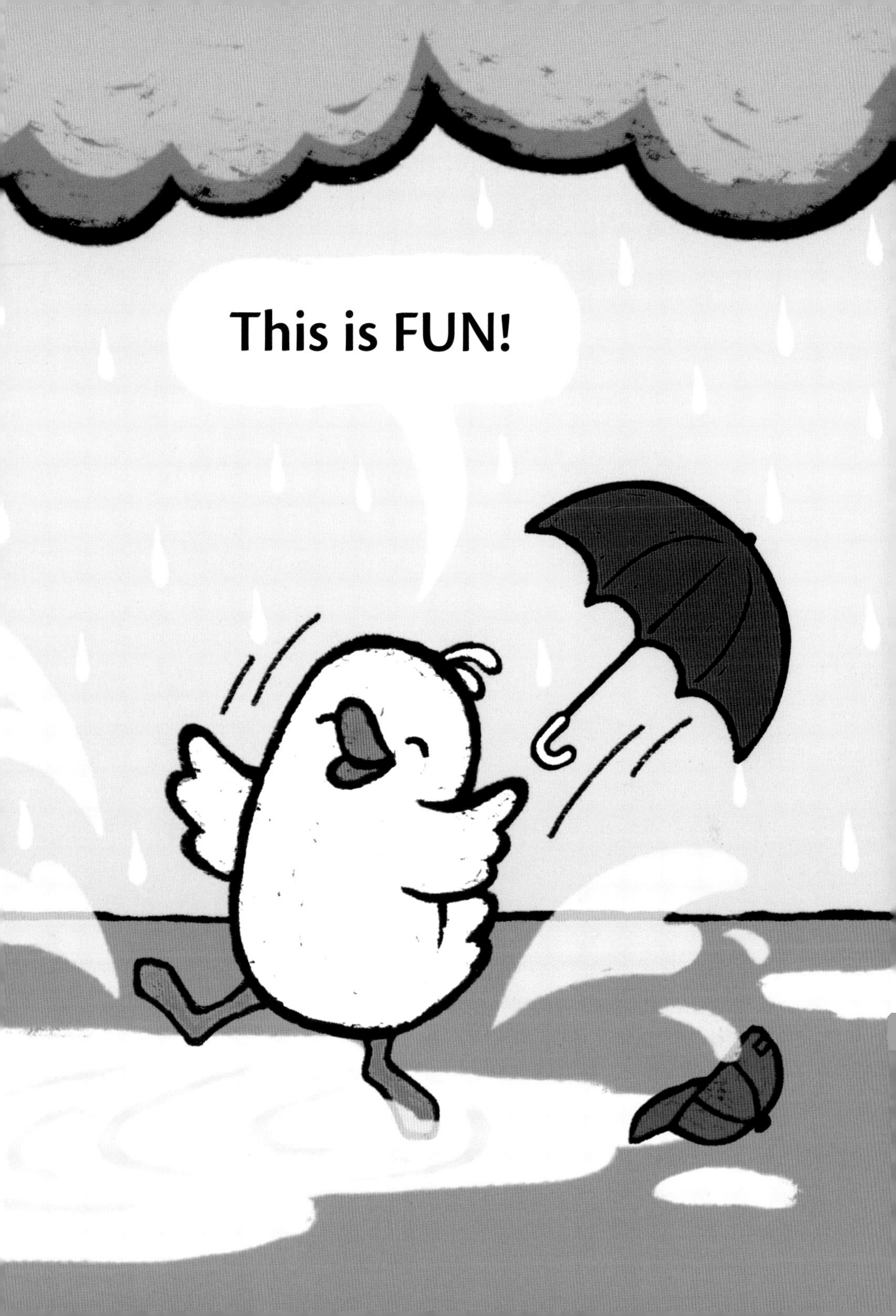
This is FUN!

TODAY is a perfect day for a picnic. The sun is out!
But there is no rain!

Two

I Think I Forgot Something!

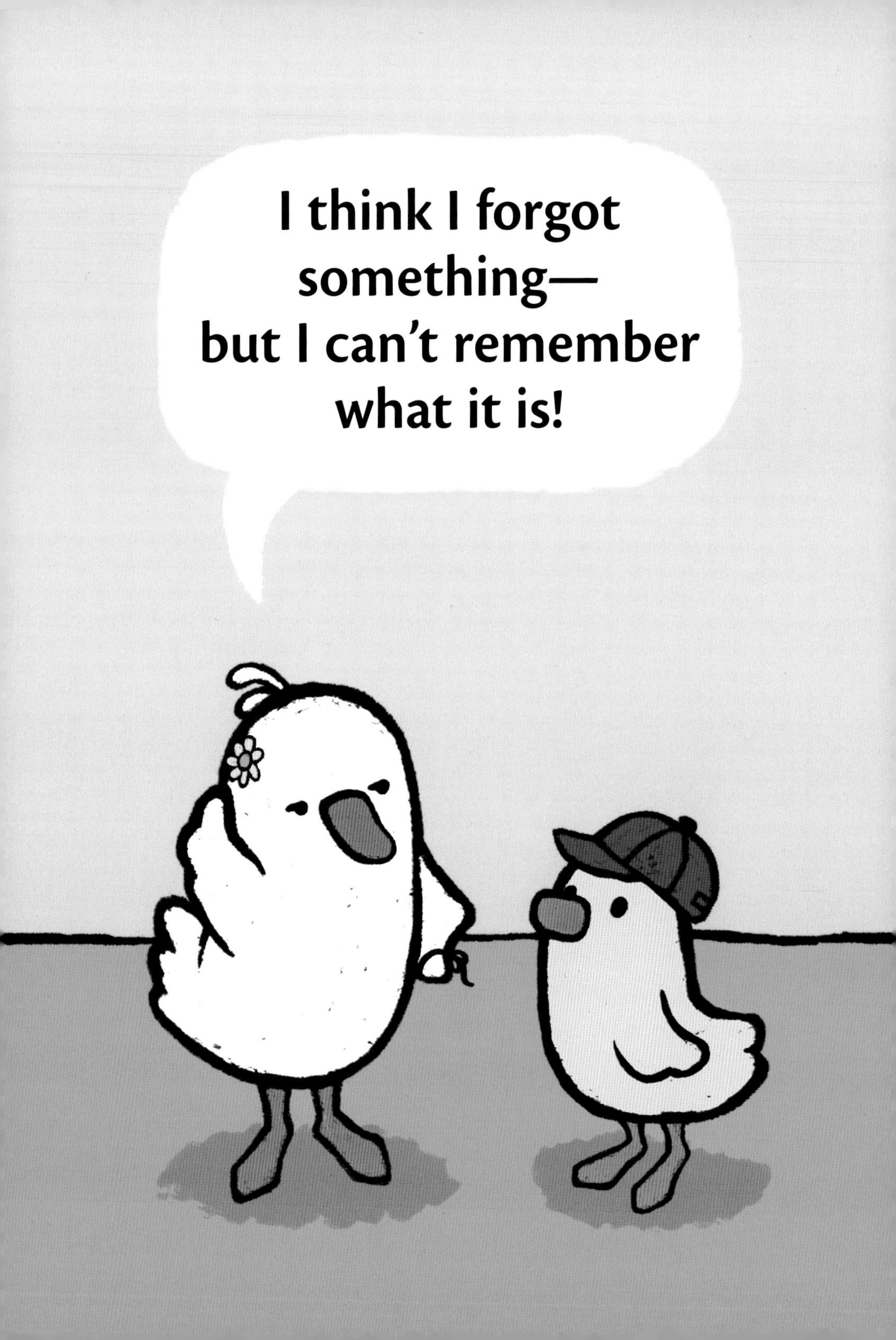
I think I forgot something—but I can't remember what it is!

Maybe walking will work. Think, Big Duck, think!

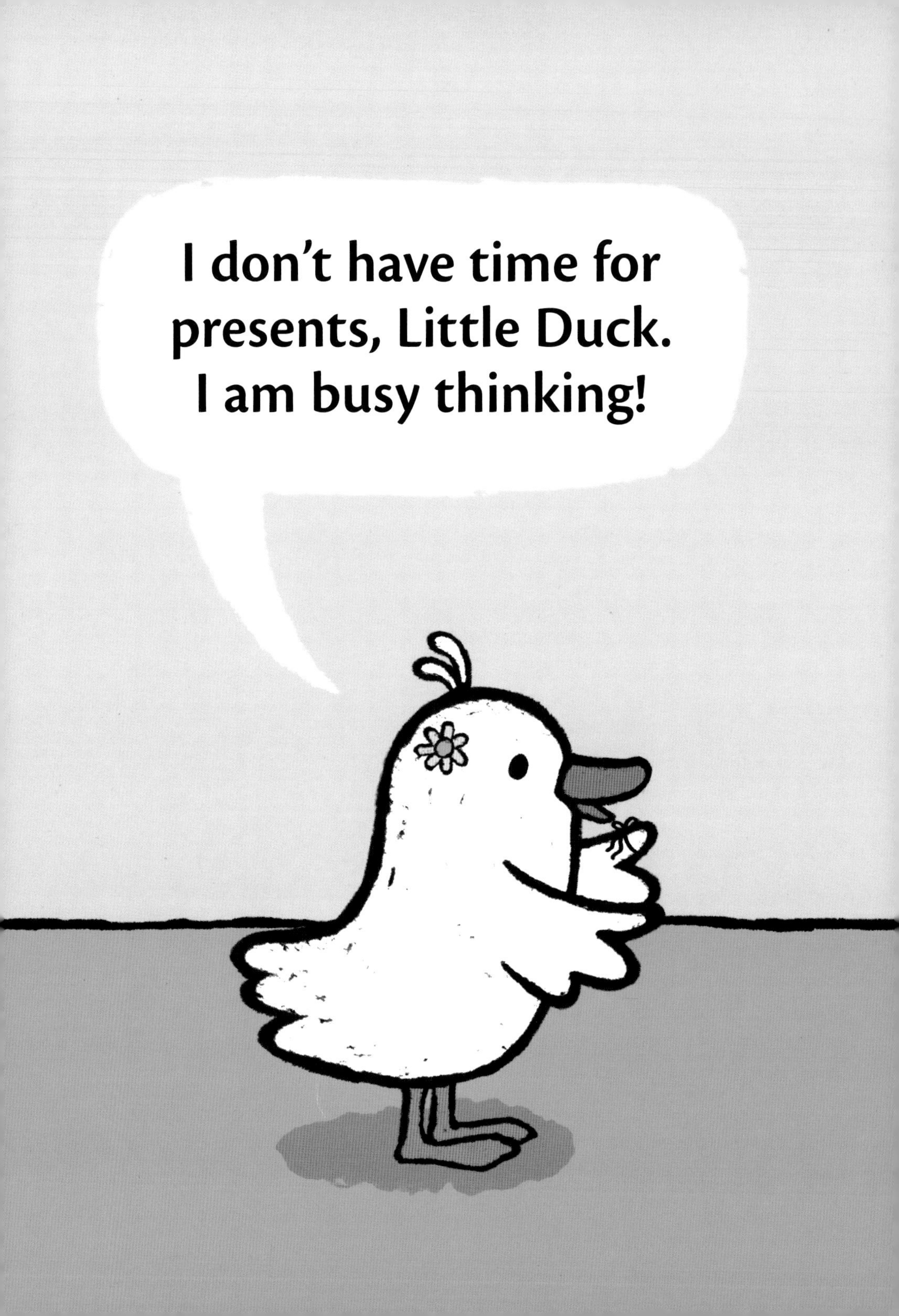
I don't have time for presents, Little Duck. I am busy thinking!

It is a big day—
but what is it?

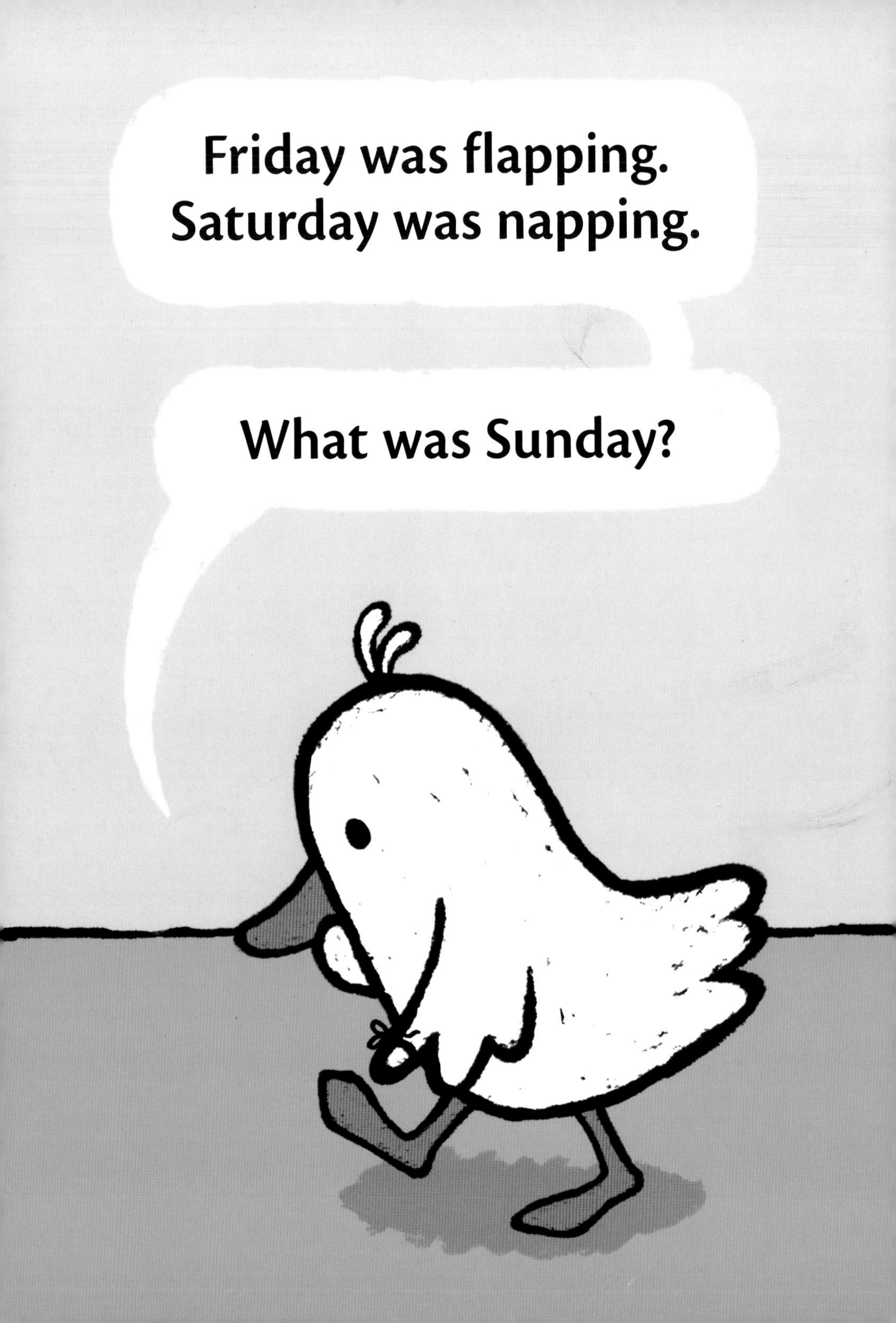
Friday was flapping.
Saturday was napping.
What was Sunday?

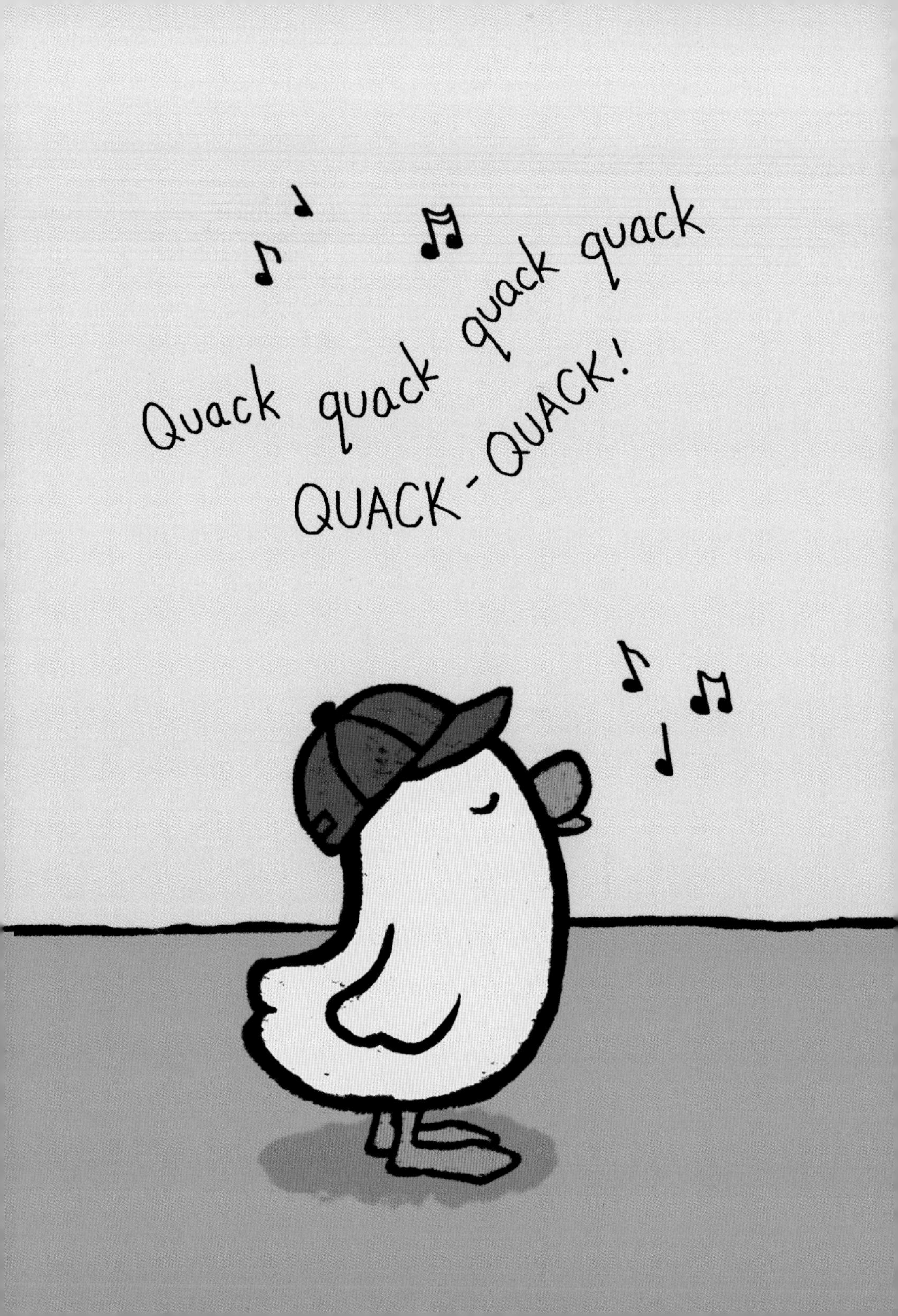
Quack quack quack quack
QUACK-QUACK!

WAIT!
I put this string on my finger to remind me of something.
For Porcupine

Three

The Campout

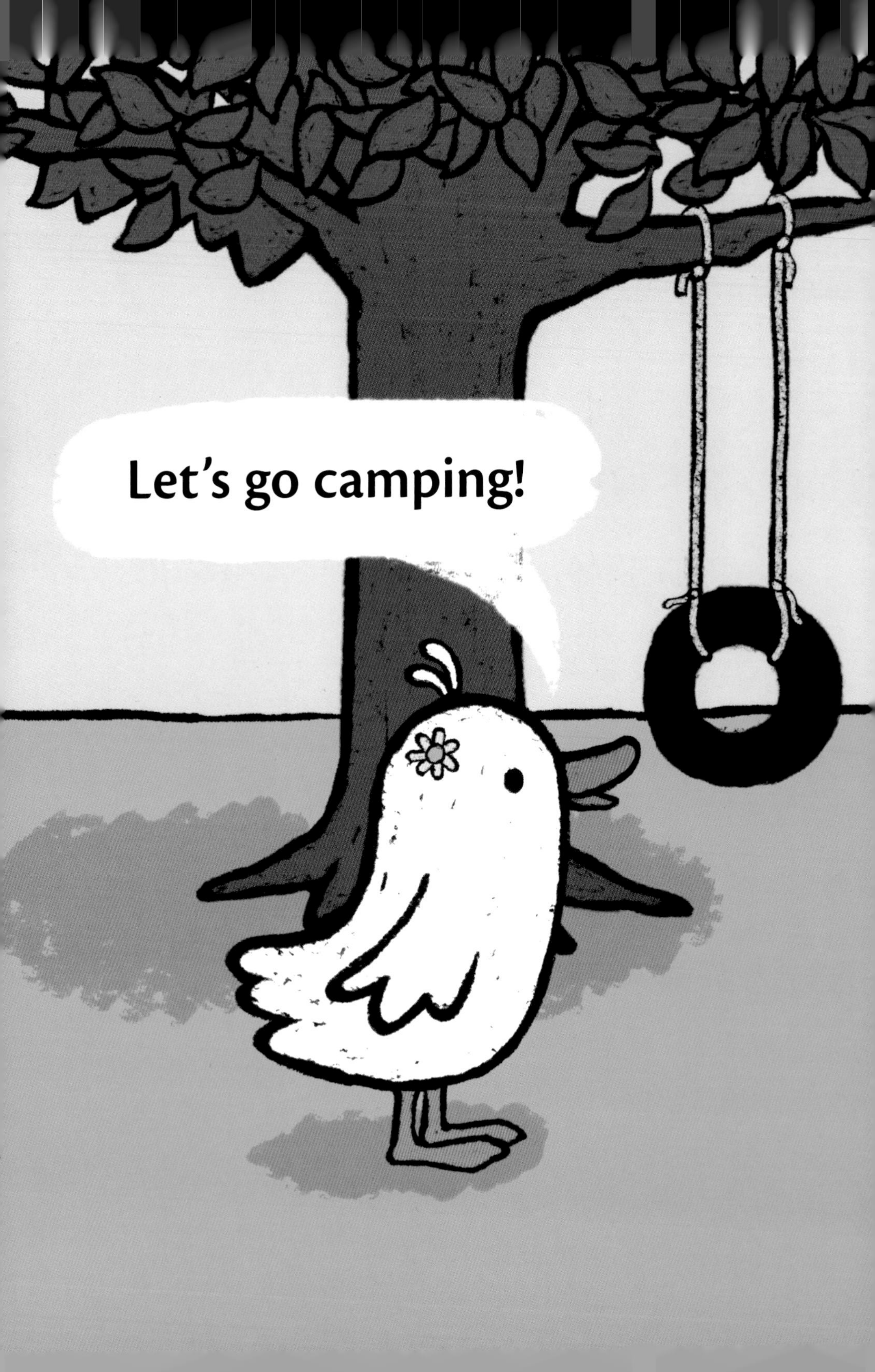
Let's go camping!

But I don't
know how.

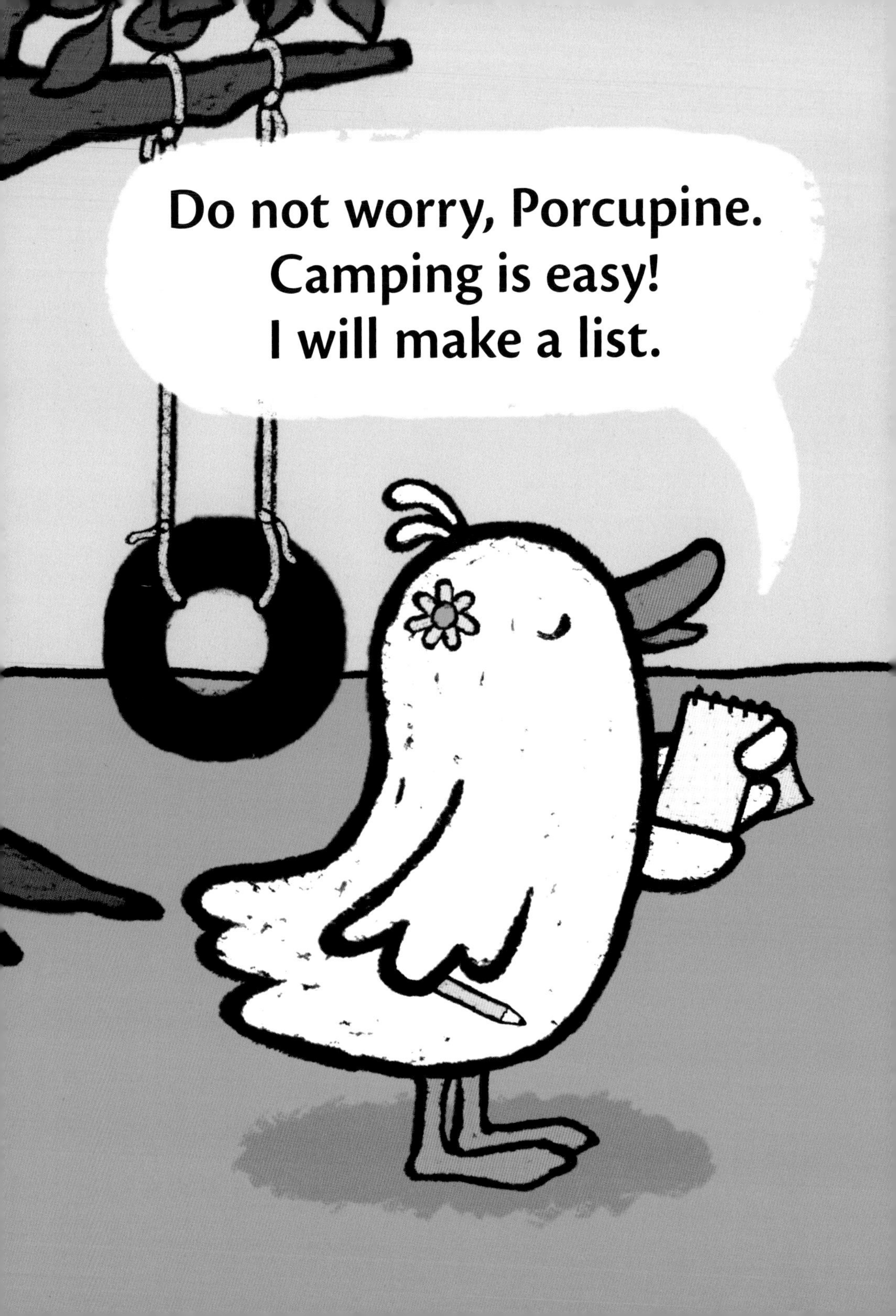
Do not worry, Porcupine.
Camping is easy!
I will make a list.

26. fishing pole
27. pots
28. pans
29. sat

59. lamp
60. root beer
61. toaster
62. ch

This is a long list, Big Duck!
You can't be too prepared, Porcupine!

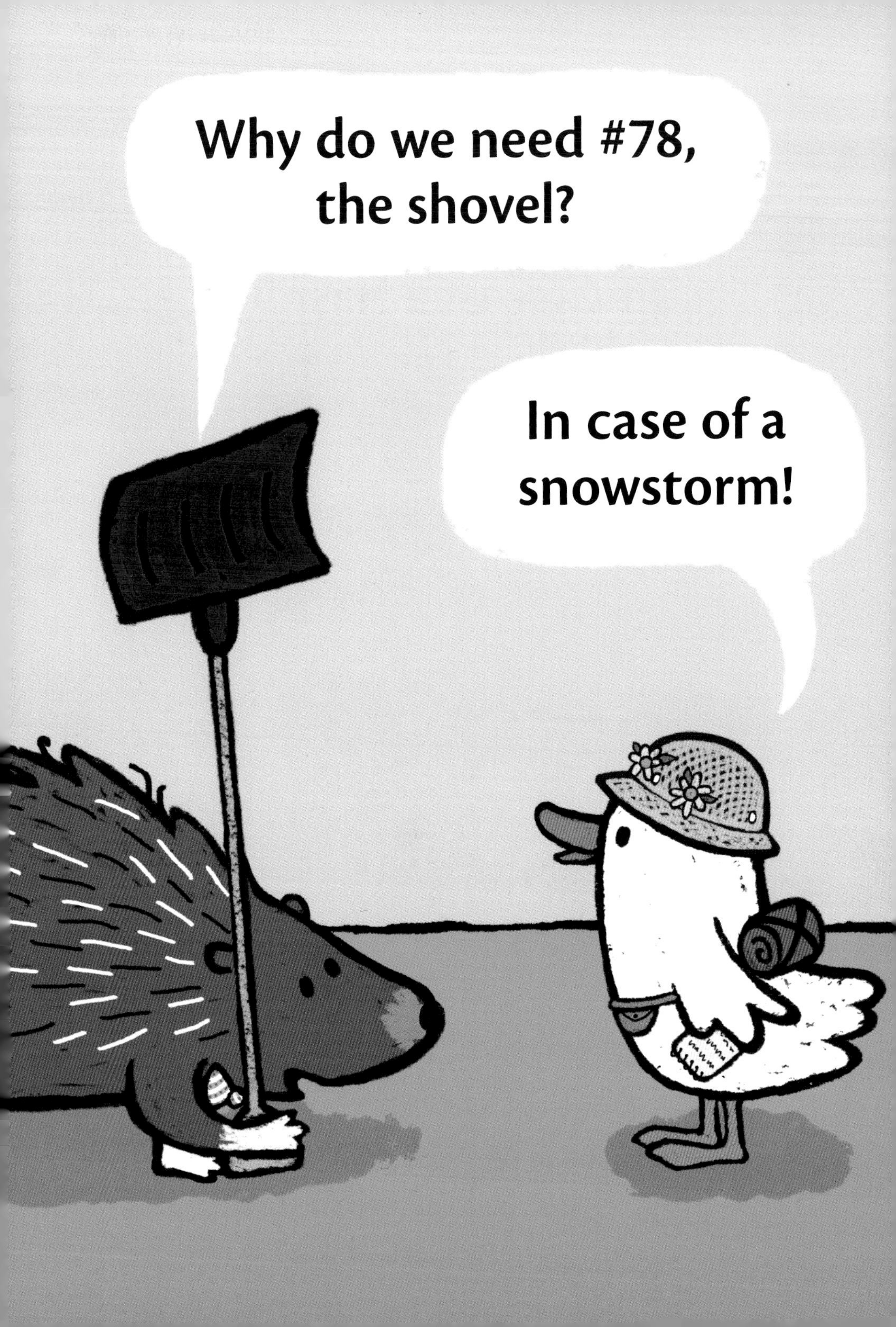
Why do we need #78, the shovel?
In case of a snowstorm!

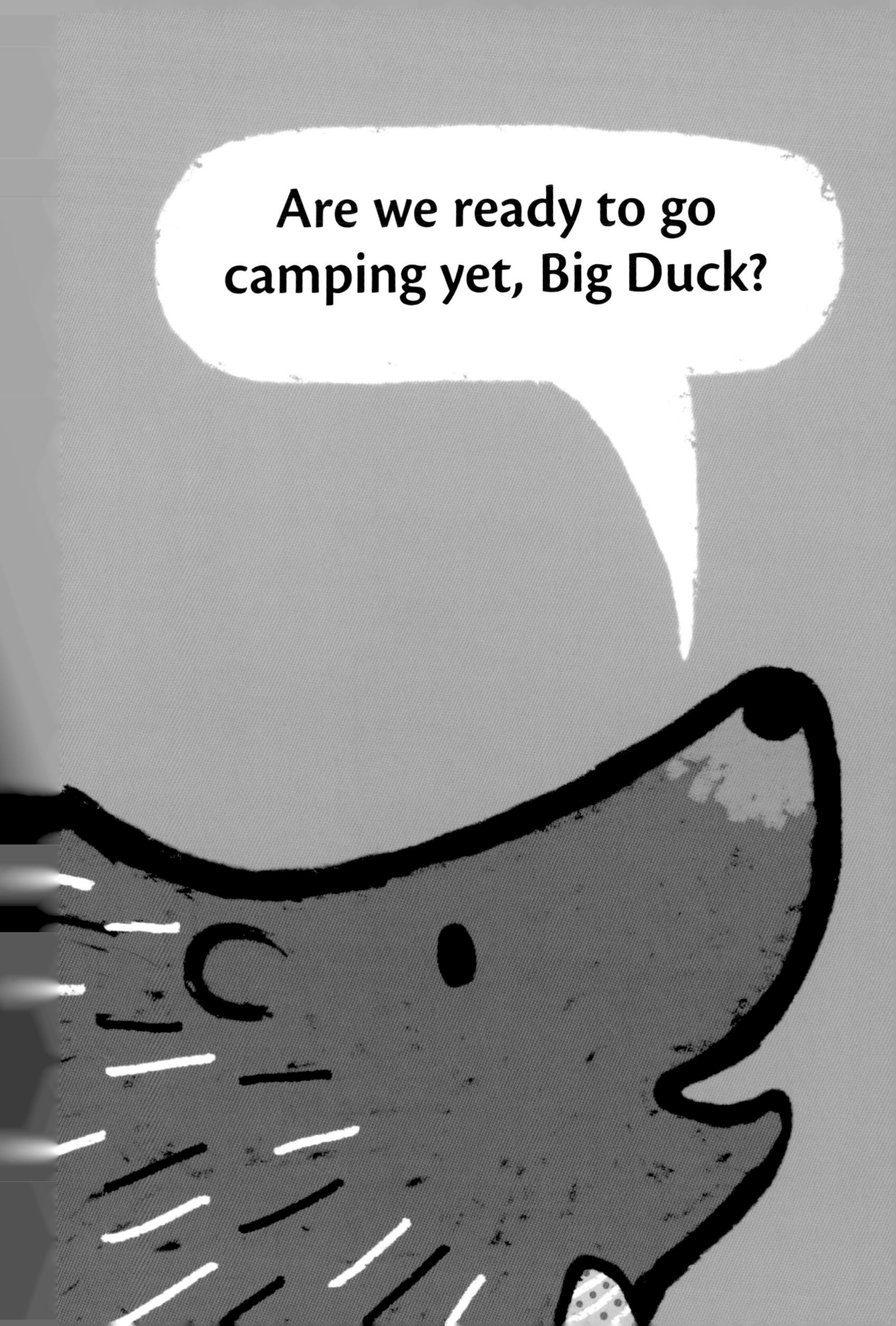
Are we ready to go camping yet, Big Duck?

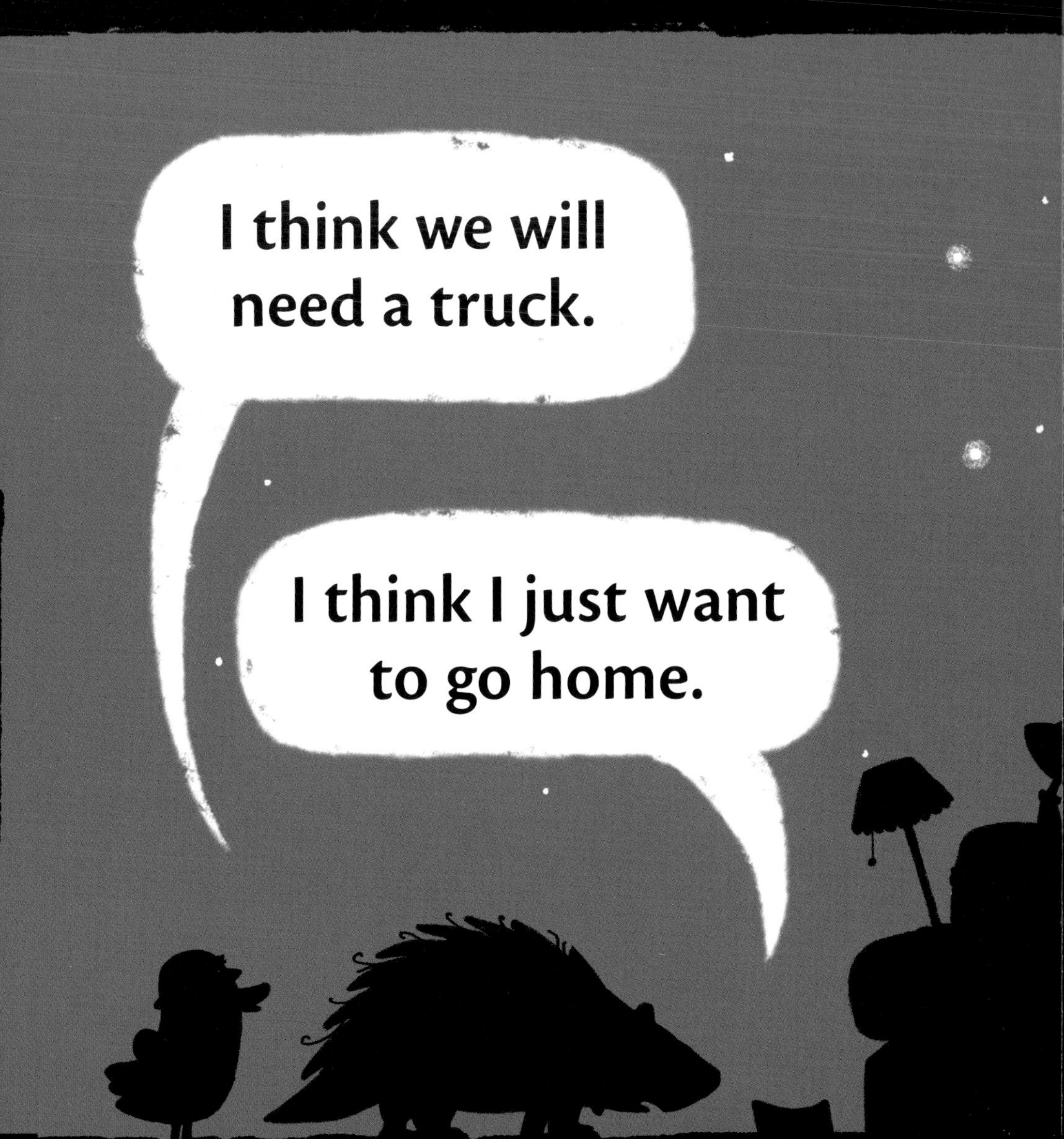
I think we will need a truck.
I think I just want to go home.

Little Duck is CAMPING!
Of course he is, because he has item #100 . . .

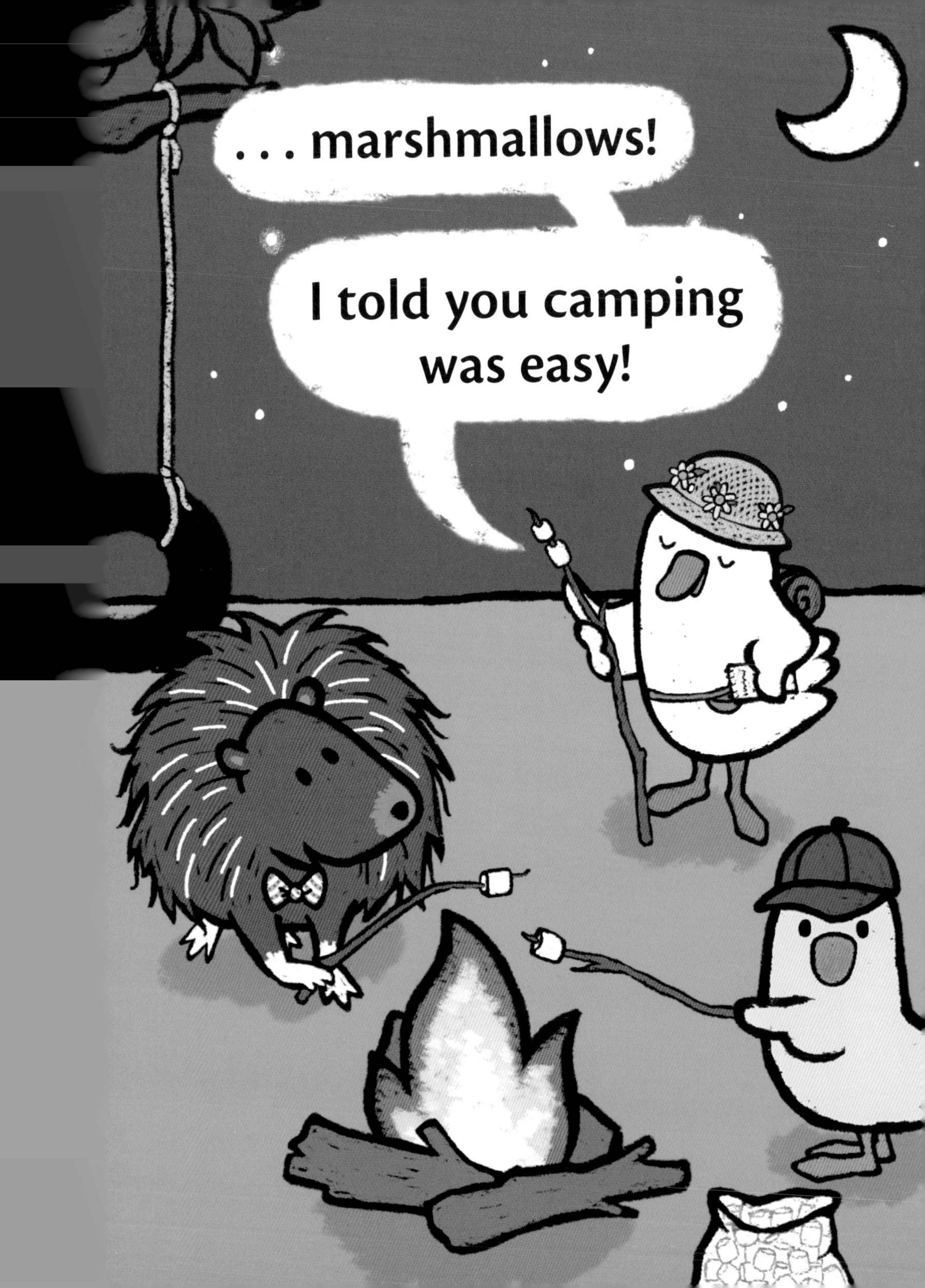
. . . marshmallows!
I told you camping was easy!